Tickly Christmas, Wibbly Pig!

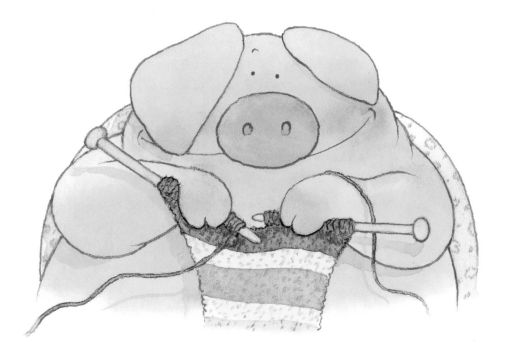

Mick Inkpen

Hodder
Children's
Books

A division of Hodder Headline Limited

Wibbly Pig has a
Christmas scarf,
made last year,
especially for him,
by Big Aunt Larlie.
So it is very special.

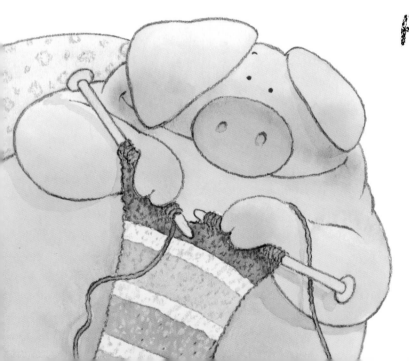

He doesn't like it
very much.

Other Wibbly Pig books:
Wibbly Pig likes bananas
Wibbly Pig can dance
Wibbly Pig is happy
Wibbly Pig makes pictures
Wibbly Pig opens his presents
Wibbly Pig makes a tent
The Wibbly Pig Collection
Everyone Hide from Wibbly Pig
In Wibbly's Garden
Is it bedtime Wibbly Pig?

First published in 2005
by Hodder Children's Books,
a division of Hodder Headline Limited,
338 Euston Road, London NW1 3BH

Copyright © 2005 Mick Inkpen

The right of Mick Inkpen to be identified as
the author of this Work has been
asserted by him in accordance with the
Copyright, Designs and Patents Act 1988.

ISBN 0340 893508

2 4 6 8 10 9 7 5 3 1

A CIP catalogue record for this book
is available from the British Library.

Printed in China

Wibbly has
special gloves too.
One of them
arrived the
Christmas before last.

And the other arrived
the Christmas
before that.
Can you guess
who made them?

Big Aunt Larlie.

The Christmas before
all of these Christmases,
Wibbly Pig was just
a little, baby piglet.
And he looked
like this.

And Big Aunt Larlie
was to blame.

Wibbly's special scarf
and gloves are tickly.

Itch!
Ooch!
Ouch!

But when it's cold outside,
and snow has fallen,
Wibbly Pig must wear his
special scarf, and his special
gloves. It's expected.

It is ten days before Christmas, and Wibbly Pig is helping to put up the Christmas decorations.

This year, for the very first time, Big Aunt Larlie is coming to stay.

Big Aunt Larlie has bought herself some balls of wool – more balls of wool than usual.

Click! Clack! go her knitting needles.

Something very special is on the way.

Oh no.

Wibbly's friends do not have aunties like Big Aunt Larlie.

'I wonder what I will get this year,' says Wibbly Pig. 'I have tickly gloves. I have a tickly scarf.'

'I know!' says Spotty Pig. 'A tickly hat!'

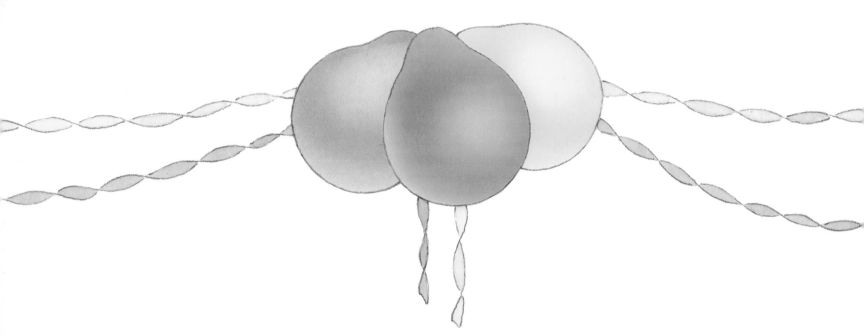

It's Christmas Eve and
Wibbly Pig is investigating
Christmas parcels.
Itch! Ooch! Ouch!
The tree is tickly too!
Just like the hat he will
get from Big Aunt Larlie.

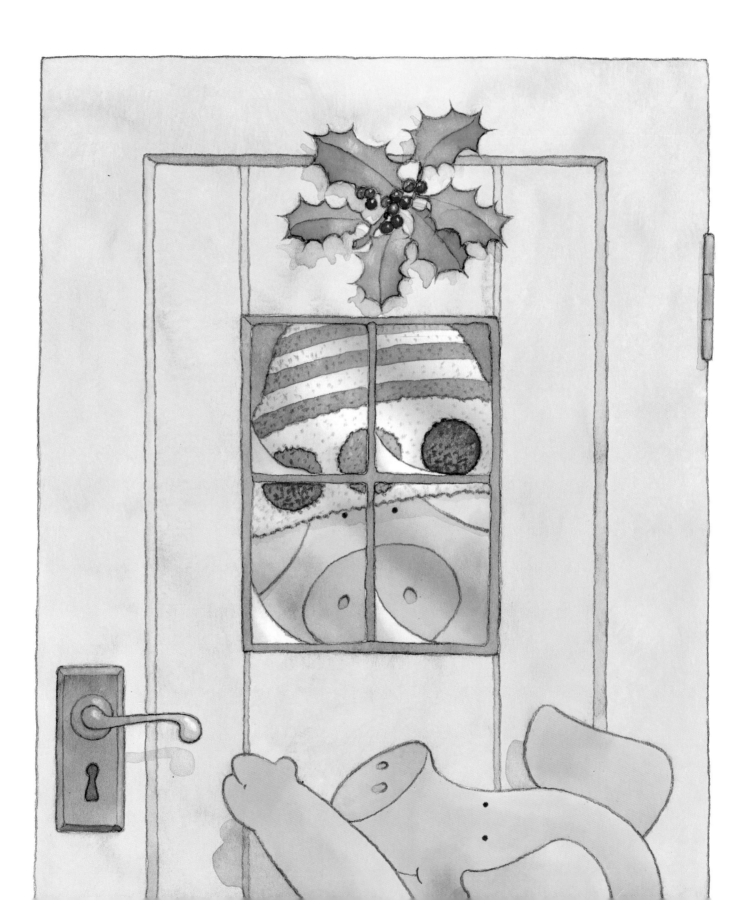

Ding! Dong! goes
the doorbell.
It's Big Aunt Larlie,
come to stay.

Wibbly Pig is
surprised.
'Aunt Larlie!' he says.
'You're wearing my
present!'

Big Aunt Larlie laughs.
'No I'm not, Wibbly
dear!' she says. 'This year
I've made a special
Christmas outfit for
myself!

This is YOUR present!'

There is no tickly
hat for Wibbly Pig!
Oh dear!
What a shame!

This year
Wibbly Pig
will have to
make do with...

...whooosh!

A toboggan!

Happy Christmas, Wibbly Pig!